SIXTH SUNDAY

Written by Arielle Haughee

Illustrated by Anastasiya Yanovskaya

ORANGE BLOSSOM PUBLISHING

Maitland, Florida

Illustrations created digitally, all text hand lettered
Published 2020 by Orange Blossom Publishing

Maitland, Florida
www.orangeblossombooks.com
info@orangeblossombooks.com

Interior Formatting: Autumn Skye

Hardback Edition ISBN: 978-1-949935-27-1
Paperback Edition ISBN: 978-1-949935-25-7
Digital Edition ISBN: 978-1-949935-26-4

Library of Congress Control Number: NUMBER

To my big sister Amber, for Always making things fun when we were kids. —A.H.

To my future kid, I hope every day of our lives will be like Sixth Sunday. —A.Y.

I want Mom to **BREAK** the **RULES**. Mom says she will - on the **SIXTH SUNDAY** of the month.

I know exactly what will **HAPPEN...**

She will
WIN.

Then she'll **RACE ME** to the kitchen. The first one there will get to **LAUNCH BREAKFAST.**

Sometimes
we will
MISS.

We'll DRESS each other.

When I pull out the paint supplies, Mom will demonstrate

SPLATTER ART.

We will
RUN OUT
of PAINT.

At the grocery store, Mom will zoom the cart like a **SPEEDSTER** ON the **TRACK**.

WE will All

grAb cAndy

at the check out.

When it's lunchtime,
Mom will make her
SANDWICH
TALK.

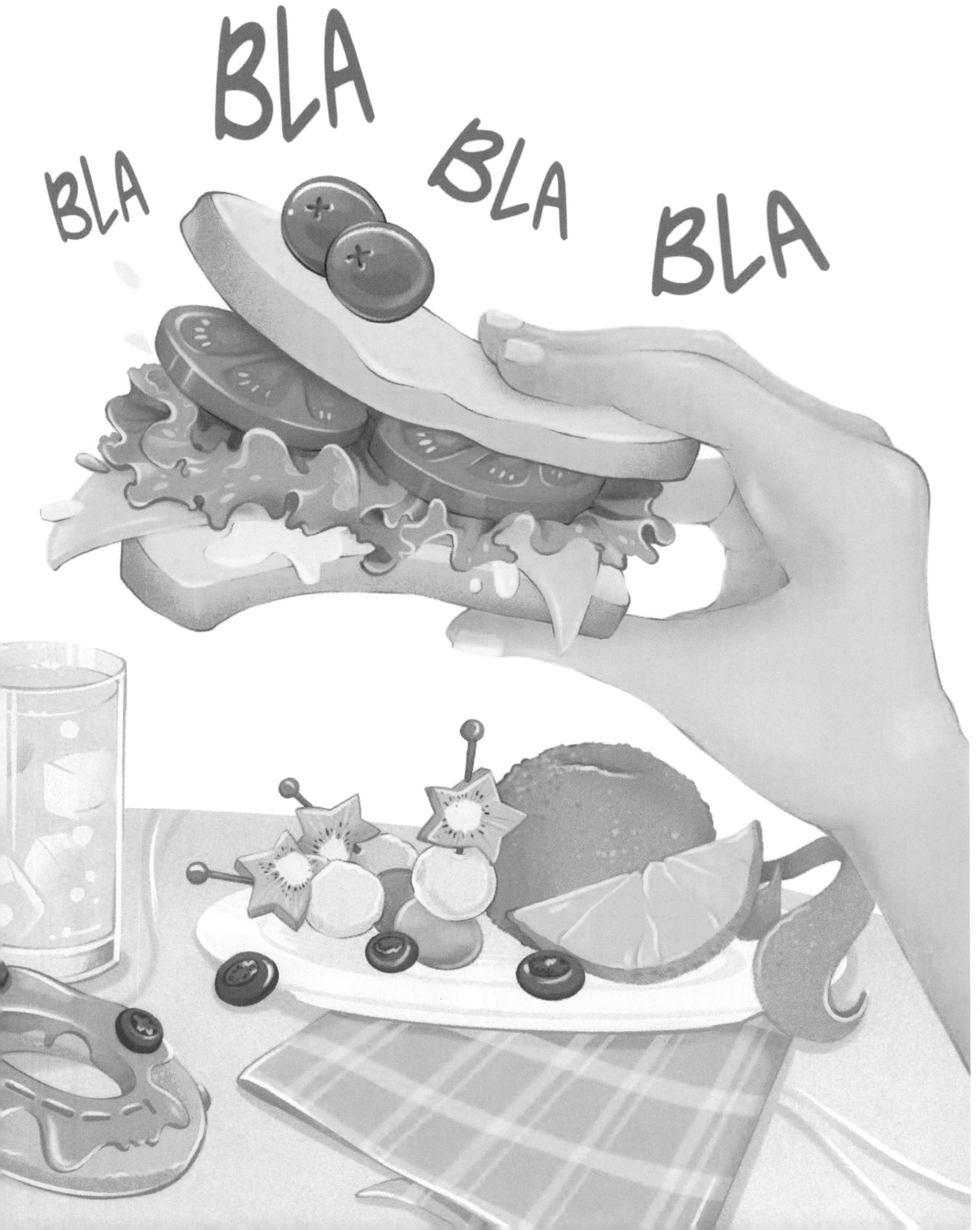
BLA
BLA
BLA
BLA

Then we'll need a FORT.

She'll lead our defense against the STRANGE INVADER.

Next we'll go outside for
BASEBALL.

So we'll make some.

Mom's will have DOUBLE WORMS.

During **BATH TIME,** Mom will make an impressive **BUBBLE BEARD.**

Together we'll conquer
PIRATE ISLAND.

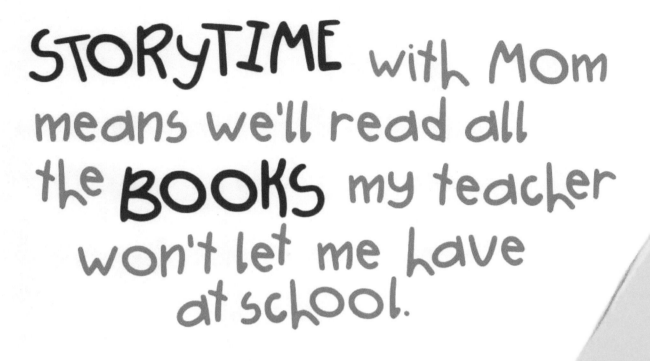

STORYTIME with Mom means we'll read all the **BOOKS** my teacher won't let me have at school.

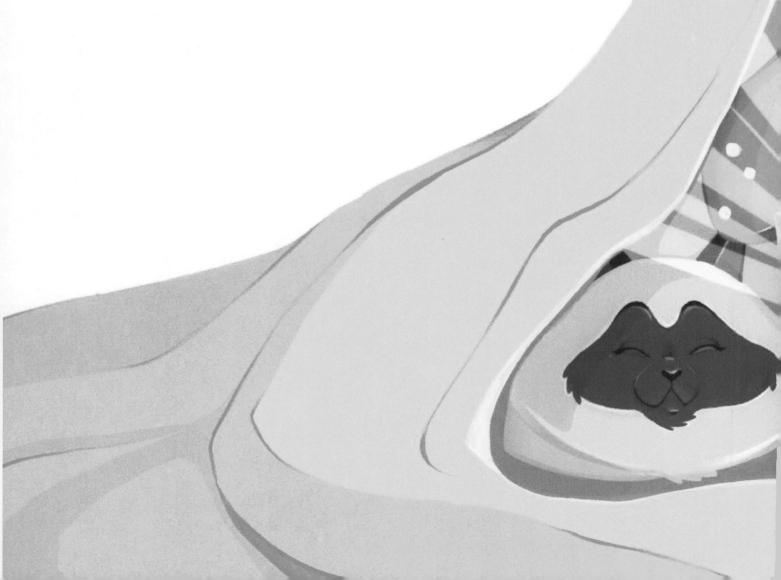

Then I'll get the POPCORN ready for MOVIE TIME.

There might be soft SNORES coming from the sofa.

I'll carry Mom to bed,
whisper a dream in her ear,
and wait for the next
SIXTH SUNDAY.

CPSIA information can be obtained
at www.ICGtesting.com
Printed in the USA
BVHW061117250122
627119BV00010B/1087